Little Vasco's Spice Adventure (children's picture books)

ISBN: 978-93-3427-584-1 (Paperback)

ISBN: 978-93-7062-278-4 (Hardback)

Contact

saharasagar@gmail.com

www.sagarkadamanim.com

sagarkadam_artwork

Publisher

Books Mantra Publications
(An imprint of Clever Fox Publishing)
www.booksmantra.com

Little Vasco's Spice Adventure

Author & Illustrator
Sagar Kadam

Book Reading Instructions for Parents

Dear Parents,
To make this book a delightful blend of imagination and practical learning for your child, please prepare a small plate with a few peppercorns, cardamom pods, cloves, star anise, and a stick of cinnamon before you begin reading.

We hope you and your child enjoy Vasco's Spice Adventure!

Best regards,
Sagar Kadam
Author

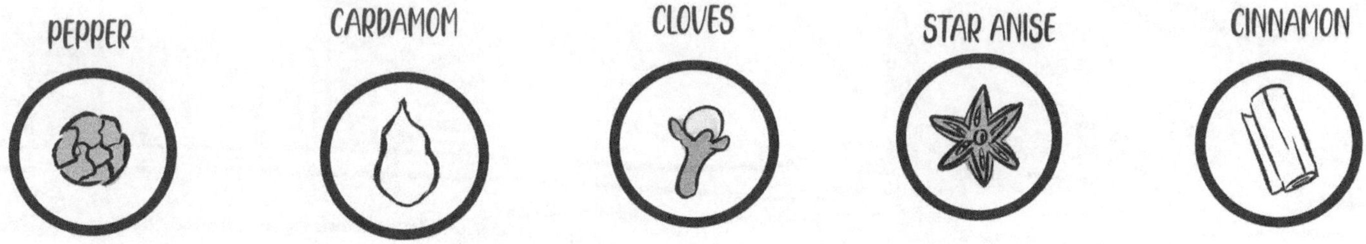

Once upon a time, deep in a faraway land, there was a magnificent kingdom.

One day, the beloved princess of the kingdom fell ill and grew very weak.

The worried King searched HIGH and LOW for a cure to heal his daughter.

A famous doctor was called in.

He said to the king, "She will get WELL only when she drinks a special remedy made from spices like...

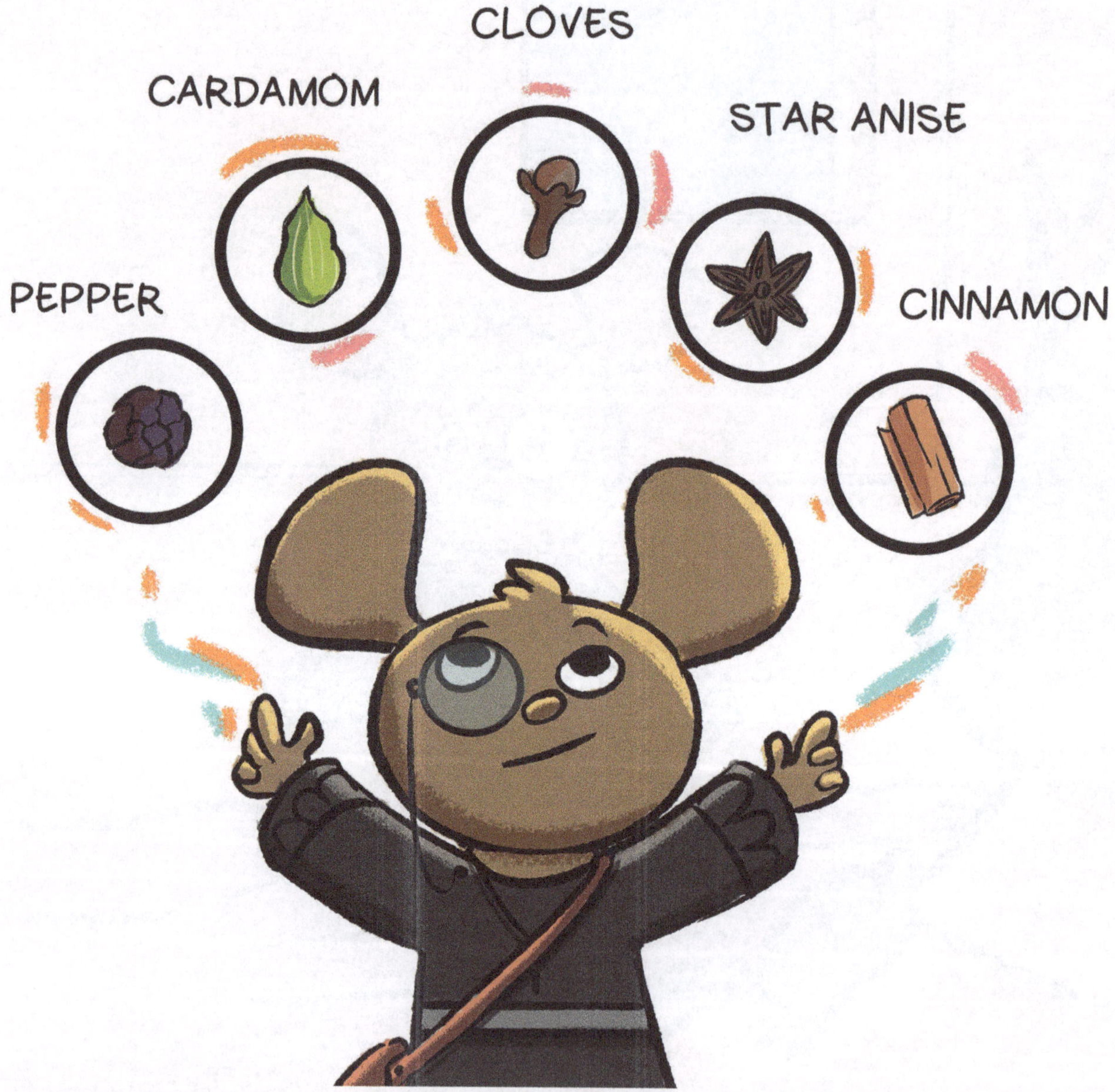

pepper, cardamom, cloves, star anise and cinnamon."

To find those rare spices, someone had to cross dangerous oceans and go deep into Indian forests.

The King summoned a brave and adventurous explorer...

...called Vasco, who was known for his fearless nature and adventurous SPIRIT.

Vasco accepted the KING's challenge to save the beloved princess...

...and set off on a LONG journey across stormy seas.

He battled MIGHTY waves, packed with unexpected encounters.

He finally reached the FOREST.

After walking a long way, Vasco found his first SPICE on a black pepper plant.

Some of the peppercorns were still on the vine, while some had fallen to the ground.

Vasco hid and watched.

A few walking and talking guardian peppercorns seemed to be protecting the tree.

Vasco stepped forward and attacked the tree guardians!

He grabbed the FRESH peppercorns with all his strength, scattering some of them around.

Then he moved on to find the other spices.

Next, he saw a clove tree. It also had some guardian cloves that could walk and talk.

Vasco did what he had done before:

He attacked the tree, plucked a small clove flower bud, and left the place in a huge mess!

He did the same to get the cinnamon,

Then again, to grab the cardamom...

...and finally, to fetch the star anise,

creating CHAOS each time.

Vasco took all the spices and went back to the kingdom to save the princess.

He handed them to the doctor, but upon inspection, the doctor said they were not useful: only DRIED spices could save the princess!

Vasco was surprised to hear this and didn't know what to do as he had left a BIG mess in the forest.

Seeing that the princess had grown weaker, Vasco decided to go back and bring the fully dried spices.

Upon returning, he didn't find any spices.

He had ruined everything by attacking the spices one by one,

trying to take them forcefully.

He felt sad because now he couldn't save the princess!

He felt helpless and his eyes filled with tears.

One peppercorn was watching him closely.

At first, it was angry at Vasco for destroying the forest, but it wanted to know what had made him cry.

Nervously, the peppercorn asked Vasco what had happened.

"You got what you wanted by ruining our home. Why are you crying?"

Vasco felt awful and said, “I am SORRY for what I did. The princess is really sick and she needed all the spices to be cured, but none of them were dried!"

The peppercorn felt sad hearing about the princess and said:

"If you had asked us nicely and politely in the first place, we would have been happy to help.

We are here to provide remedies and make food delicious.

Taking things forcefully was NOT right."

Then, the peppercorn said, "Follow me."

It walked alongside Vasco and took him to the place where all the ruined spices lay scattered.

They were angry when they saw Vasco...

...but after hearing the story of the princess, they forgave him.

Vasco apologised for his actions and promised to be HUMBLE and KIND from then on.

All the dried spices agreed to go with him to save the princess.

When Vasco returned once more, the doctor made a soup with all the spices...

...and gave it to the princess.

She felt much better after eating the doctor's SPECIAL soup.

And brave little Vasco - he had learned a valuable lesson about humility and the importance of asking for help politely.

True bravery isn't just about strength - it comes from within, and his heart was now FULL of courage and kindness.